Chasing the CROWN

By Wendy Loggia

Based on "Princess Protection Program," Teleplay by Annie DeYoung

Based on the Story by David Morgasen and Annie DeYoung

DISNEP PRESS

New York

Printed in the United States of America
First Edition
1 3 5 7 9 10 8 6 4 2
Library of Congress Control Number on file.
ISBN 978-1-4231-2297-5

For more Disney Press fun, visit www.disneybooks.com
Visit DisneyChannel.com

Chapter 1

Carter Mason sighed as she looked at all the clothes strewn around her room. Being organized was not one of her best qualities. Especially when it came to packing. *Especially* when she had to leave for the airport in exactly twenty-seven minutes!

"Okay," Carter said. "If I bring the black jeans, then I need to bring the purple top and the tan sweater with the crocheted belt. But if I'm bringing the tan sweater, then I should really bring my white linen shirt and the dark blue jeans. But they need to be washed. Scratch the dark blue jeans. Now I still need to bring something I can wear to a fancy dinner. Or two. Or three."

Carter blew out her breath, her hands on her hips. Her suitcase had seemed so *big* when she first started tossing things into it. But now, it looked crazily small—and very overstuffed. Dad is not going to be happy, she thought. She knew he was waiting in the living room with his black duffel and his laptop, all ready to go. She shot a guilty eye over at her backpack, wondering if the airline would count that as a carry-on. It was bulging with binders, textbooks, highlighters, a novel for English class, her flash drive, and a ragged gray sweatshirt.

I hope I didn't forget anything at school, she thought, biting her lip. Math, English, French, a paper for U.S. History . . . Then she smiled. Forget history class. She'd be getting a real-life history lesson in Washington, D.C.!

Her best friend, Queen Rosalinda, was returning to the United States for her first official state visit. Rosie would spend a week meeting with other royal dignitaries and heads of state, attending fancy dinners, and taking in the sights of the country's capital. She had invited Carter and Mr. Mason to attend the dinners as her VSGs—Very Special Guests. After all they'd done for her, she said it was the least she could do.

Carter shook her head, amused. Sometimes she still couldn't believe it had all really happened.

Not too long ago, Carter had been surprised—and, she had to admit, a little annoyed—when her father had brought some of his work home with him. Literally.

Most people thought that Joe Mason was a pretty simple guy. To them, he was the proprietor of Joe's Bait Shack, a full-service tackle shop in Lake Monroe, Louisiana. But

running the bait shop wasn't Mr. Mason's *only* job. He had a side gig, too. He was a top secret agent for the Princess Protection Program, a private organization funded by royal families all around the world.

Carter hadn't always understood her father's second job. She never knew where he was going on his missions, or how long he'd be away from her. But she did know that his work saved lives. She had often wondered about the princesses her father was sworn to protect. Did they try to make the world a better place the way her dad did? Were they snobby and only interested in fashion like most of the girls she went to school with?

She didn't have to wonder for very long. One day when Mr. Mason had returned home from a mission with a princess in tow, Carter got a front-row seat to living with a royal.

Princess Rosalinda Marie Montoya Fiore of the small nation of Costa Luna had been rescued by Carter's dad when her country was taken over. The dictator of Costa Estrella, General Kane, believed that his country and Costa Luna should be joined together and that he should be the sole ruler. Rosalinda's mother, Sophia, vehemently disagreed. And so when General Kane declared himself president of both countries, Sophia remained calm and strong. She had already alerted the Princess Protection Program. Rosalinda was whisked away to the safety of the Masons' lakeside cabin in Louisiana while things settled down in Costa Luna.

Rosalinda had been disguised as a regular American teen named Rosie González. And Carter was the one who had to show Rosie how to blend in. At first, things had not gone well.

Carter thought being a princess was silly and superficial, consisting of wearing ball gowns and waving a lot. Rosie had to learn how to live without being waited on hand and foot by a staff of servants. But once Carter got to know Rosie, she realized there was more to being a princess than she had ever imagined. In just a few weeks, Rosie became one of Carter's best friends.

When order was restored in Costa Luna, Princess Rosalinda went home for her official coronation ceremony. Now Carter felt a surge of pride whenever she thought of Rosie. Her best friend was already realizing their shared dream of doing something important with their lives.

Carter was looking forward to seeing Rosie again. It had been a few weeks since she and her father had returned home from Rosie's coronation ceremony in Costa Luna. Carter's days were filled with school, homework, and her job at the Bait Shack. When the VSG passes arrived in the mail, Carter had shrieked with joy. Her best friend knew how to dole out the royal treatment. And in only a few hours, Carter would be stepping off the plane in D.C. to have dinner with the queen.

"If I can ever get my suitcase shut," Carter muttered, staring down at the piles of clothes that littered every corner of her room. She tossed aside a pair of flannel boxers and lifted the scarf that was on her desk covering up her new silver cell phone. "And I only have twenty-one minutes!"

There was only one thing to do in this situation. Carter punched in the number on her phone's keypad that only a select handful of private citizens had access to.

She hated to bother Rosie—after all, she was the ruler of a country now! But this was an emergency of the most serious kind.

A fashion emergency.
She began typing furiously.

> **Baitgirl:** serius trble
> here!!!!!!!!! cant decide wht 2
> bring. can u help me? please??

A few minutes later a text message came back from Rosie.

> **Hrhqueenrosalinda:** I am sure
> what you have selected is fine.
> Do not worry, Carter.

Carter snorted. Easy for her to say, she thought. Rosie had probably been on hundreds of official state visits over the years as part of the royal family of Costa Luna. But this was Carter's first—and possibly only—one. She didn't want to look out of place. She frowned at the sight of a purple flip-flop on the carpet. Had she packed the other one?

> **Baitgirl:** r u sure i can wear flip-flops with my dress???

> **Hrhqueenrosalinda:** That would depend. A dress to sightsee in? Or a dress to have tea in?

> **Baitgirl:** um . . . like a dress 4 the ball?

> **Hrhqueenrosalinda:** You are so funny, Carter!

> **Baitgirl:** is that a no???

Small beads of sweat dotted her forehead as she waited for Rosie's response. Carter checked her phone display . . . she

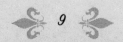

only had fifteen minutes! She heard her father cough in the living room. Great, she thought. Dad's watching the clock, too.

Just then she heard a familiar *ping*. A new message!

Hrhqueenrosalinda: Yes, Carter. That is a no. As in, no flip-flops at the ball. What about those pretty gold heels you love?

Carter peered under her bed. She was pretty sure that's where she had last seen those heels. . . . But all she found were some dirty socks, a baseball, and some crumpled papers. She hurried over to look in her closet. She kicked a soccer ball out of the way and was just reaching for a bunch of sweatpants when she spotted a gold toe shimmering next to her galoshes. "Yes!" she exclaimed as she grabbed the shoe and quickly found its match. "One outfit done, anyway."

Baitgirl: gold heels, check! :)
bt wht if i 4get somethn???

Hrhqueenrosalinda: Do not worry!
Mr. E. will be on call for any
fashion emergencies.

A wave of relief swept over Carter. Mr. E. was Mr. Elegante, Rosie's royal dress designer. Knowing that they could rely on him made Carter feel a lot more secure. He'd never let me look ridiculous, she thought, smiling to herself.

Ping!

Hrhqueenrosalinda: I can't wait
to see you and your father! I

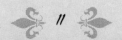

have a number of official
appearances, but definitely we
will have some time to explore
D.C. together.

Baitgirl: Yay!!!!!!! so wht do u
want 2 do 1st?

Hrhqueenrosalinda: I would like
to visit the Lincoln and
Jefferson memorials.

Baitgirl: dfntly! and maybe some
msms? my dad said there are some
really cool 1s.

Hrhqueenrosalinda: Yes, that
sounds good. I have heard that
the American history and natural
history museums are wonderful.
And maybe visiting them will
help you with your schoolwork?

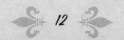

Carter laughed as she stuffed the gold shoes in her bag. Leave it to Rosie to worry about homework while they planned what to do for *fun* in D.C.

She started typing her response.

```
Baitgirl: best of all we get 2
go 2 the White House! That is
sooooooooooooooo—
```

Beep! Beep! Carter stopped typing in mid-text. Uh-oh. She looked at the clock on her nightstand. She had one minute left! She ran over to her window and swept the curtain aside. Her dad was out in front of their cabin, waiting for her in his truck. She hadn't even heard him leave the house. Why did he always have to be early for everything?

"Well, if I don't have it packed Mr. Elegante will just need to find it for me,"

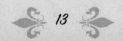

she said, shoving a wayward sock into her suitcase. Then, Carter flipped the lid closed and plopped down on top. She struggled with the zipper for just a moment before getting it to close. Then she sent one last text.

Baitgirl: time to go! bye rosie! c u soon!!

Carter tucked her cell into her backpack's front compartment, then slung the bag over her shoulder. "Oof!" she groaned. If only she didn't have all those textbooks! She kicked her soccer ball back into the closet. Then, with one final survey of her messy room, she grabbed the handle of her suitcase and wheeled it toward the door. For once, she had a good excuse for not cleaning up. She had a plane to catch!

Chapter 2

"*W*hee!" Carter shouted as she sprang onto the hotel room's queen-size bed. "I could definitely get used to this!"

The flight to D.C. had been pretty short, but the security line at the airport had taken forever. Then their plane had sat on the runway for almost an hour before actually taking off. But instead of being tired, Carter was more excited than ever.

From the moment they'd walked into the ornate hotel lobby filled with expensive-looking art, rich draperies, plush carpets, and leather furnishings, Carter had felt like she was dreaming. She ran her fingers over the sheets. "These are the softest things I've ever felt!"

She hopped off the bed and hurried through the adjoining bathroom, bursting into her father's room. "Can you believe this?" she cried.

"I have to admit, it is a step up from our usual digs," Mr. Mason said, his eyes twinkling. He had already hung up his clothes in the closet, arranged his shaving stuff on the vanity, listened to his voice mail, and set up his laptop. Now he was busy checking the latest sports highlights on the huge plasma TV that hung on the wall.

Carter left her father to his sports and scrambled back through the door to scope out the bathroom. There was a huge double-sink vanity. Next to a lighted makeup mirror was a silver tray with fancy little bottles of shampoo, conditioner, lotion, and mouthwash. "Mmm," Carter said, opening

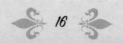

one to sniff the lavender-scented body lotion inside. Plush terry-cloth bathrobes and slippers in cloth bags hung on the backs of both bathroom doors. Mounted on the wall was another flat-screen TV, a hair dryer, and a telephone. In case I need to order a pizza while I'm in the tub, Carter thought.

But the best thing was the soap.

"Dad!" Carter shouted, popping her head back into her father's room. "You have got to see this." She held out her hand. "The soap is in the shape of the White House!"

Her dad laughed. "And soon you'll be going there. Maybe you can keep the soap as a souvenir."

"Nah. I want the real thing." Carter walked back into her room and over to the large window. She moved the heavy drapes aside. Their suite had an incredible view of Pennsylvania Avenue. And there, just as she had seen it on TV hundreds of times, was the White House, beautiful and brilliant. Carter wondered what was going on inside—if the president was making an important decision or fixing himself a turkey sandwich. Her history teacher had raved about how beautiful the grounds and gardens were, and about how remarkable it was to see the executive mansion in person.

And she was right, Carter thought, letting the drapes fall closed.

She wandered over to a dark wood cabinet and pulled on the handle. It was locked. But the tiny key to unlock it was sitting right on top. Carter turned the key and pulled the door open. Jackpot! It was fully stocked with snacks and soft drinks. "Yum! Dad," she called. "Can we eat these?" She pulled out a stack of chocolate bars and a jar filled with cashews.

Mr. Mason walked into her room and shook his head. "You'd have to work about

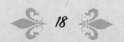

ten shifts at the Bait Shack to pay for that. Rosie and her mother are kind enough to put us up in this suite while we're here, and I don't want to take advantage of their generosity."

Carter quickly put the chocolate and nuts away and closed the cabinet. "Got it. But Dad? I am starving."

Mr. Mason looked at his watch. "Well, it's too late to go out, Carter." He picked up a leather directory from the desk and handed it to her. "Looks like we'll have to order room service."

"Really?" Carter asked, her eyes wide. "That's even better!" She opened the directory and flipped through the various hotel services until she found the all-day dining menu. "Okay, Dad. What'll it be? The organic colonial greens and shaved fennel salad? Or maybe the farm-raised Atlantic salmon with a cup of chicken rice soup?"

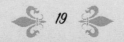

Mr. Mason patted his stomach. "How about a cheeseburger and fries?"

Carter peered at the menu. "Hmm. Guess that would be the Black Angus burger with Vermont cheddar and a side of hand-cut potatoes."

"Sold," Mr. Mason said. "How about you?"

Carter chewed on her lip. Everything sounded good, but what she really wanted was . . . "I know I'm not exactly a 'Li'l Guest,' but do you think I could get the PB & J, carrot sticks, and a fruit smoothie from the kids' menu?" She knew it was a strange order when she could've had filet mignon, Chilean sea bass, or vegetarian lasagna brought to their door. But peanut butter and jelly was classic.

"I don't see why not," her dad replied. After he placed the order, Carter started putting her stuff away in the dresser drawers. She was in the middle of folding a top when a firm knock sounded at her door.

"Wow, that was fast," Carter said, walking over to open it. But instead of a waiter with a food cart, it was Rosie!

"Hey, you!" Carter squealed, throwing her arms around her friend. "I thought you were room service!"

Rosie giggled. "I should have had them wheel me up here on a cart. I could have hidden under a silver food dome!"

Carter shook her head. "Nope. The crown wouldn't fit." She stepped back to take Rosie in. "You are in total queen mode," she said with a grin. It still amazed Carter how Rosie could go from looking like a completely average teenager to a sophisticated, elegant queen. Tonight Rosie wore a deep blue gown with a pleated bustier and cap sleeves and long, cream-colored gloves. Her hair was pulled back into a low chignon, and a diamond-encrusted crown sparkled on her head. "I didn't think we'd get to see each other tonight."

Rosie shrugged. "The orchestra performance I attended at the Kennedy Center ended ahead of schedule. So I decided to see if you were still awake!"

"Like I could sleep. This place is amazing!" Carter opened the door wider to let her friend in. "Hey, Jorge. Hi, Victor," she said, waving to the two men in dark suits who stood a respectful but close distance from Rosie. They were part of Rosie's personal security detail. Carter had met them at the coronation festivities in Costa Luna.

"Hello, Carter." They nodded to Mr. Mason, who had stepped over to the doorway. "All good?"

Carter's dad nodded. "Gave the room a full security sweep when we checked in," he said.

"Okay then. We'll be outside if you need

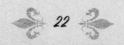

22

us," the guards said as Rosie walked into the room and gave Mr. Mason a hug.

"It is good to see you, Major Mason," Rosie said, smiling at him.

"And you, Your Highness."

She waved away the formalities with her hand. "Please. Just Rosie."

"You got it, Rosie," Mr. Mason said, heading back to his room. "I'll let you girls be then."

Rosie bent down to take off her high heels. "My favorite part of wearing these is taking them off," she joked, looping the straps over her finger.

"I've got something that's going to make us a whole lot comfier," Carter said.

A few moments later, Carter and Rosie were wrapped in the plush hotel bathrobes and sprawled out on the bed. Rosie's crown sat on top of the tissue box on the night-stand.

"So how is everyone back at Lake Monroe High School?" Rosie asked, a warm expression on her face. "I have such fond memories."

"Oh, like when Chelsea and Brooke tricked you at the yogurt shop and you were covered head to toe in dairy product?" Carter asked tartly.

Rosie shook her head. "They didn't mean real harm, Carter. And it was kind of funny now that I think about it." She smiled. "Is Ed still filming everything he sees?"

Carter nodded. "He entered a short-film contest. I think he has a good chance of winning."

Rosie smiled. "That is wonderful."

Carter caught her up on all the high school gossip and then rolled onto her elbow. "Okay. Now that you know what's going on in Louisiana, you've got to fill me in on what's going to happen here in D.C. Who we're going to meet, where we're going to be . . . I don't want to make any huge mistakes."

Rosie smiled. "Do not worry, Carter. You'll be a perfect VSG."

Carter laughed. "If you say so, Your Highness. Now . . . details!"

"Well, the most important event is the dinner tomorrow at the White House, because it involves several heads of state," Rosie explained. "In addition to myself, there will be King George and his wife, Queen Marie, the rulers of Pacardi, a remote European country; Nicholas and Pavlos, two brothers who are princes; and Her Royal Highness, the Crown Princess Alice Catherine of Scandia. Not to mention many politicians, including senators, governors, campaign donors, and definitely a journalist or two."

"Two royal brothers, hmm?" Carter wagged her eyebrows. "Wouldn't it be awesome if I got to sit between them at dinner?" Carter closed her eyes, imagining herself telling everyone back home about tall, dark, and handsome Prince Nicholas. . . .

"Chelsea would have a cow if I came home with a boyfriend who's a prince," she said. "I mean, not that I could actually bring him home, but—" Carter broke off as Rosie dissolved into a fit of giggles. "What's so funny?"

"Oh, just the thought of you batting your eyelashes at Prince Nicholas and Prince Pavlos." Rosie wiped away a tear. "Prince Charmings? Uh-uh. More like Prince Windbags. They're old, bald, and like nothing more than to talk about themselves. But if that's what you want . . ."

Carter playfully punched Rosie in the arm. "Gross! Forget I ever said that."

Rosie rubbed her bicep. "You know, I *could* have you arrested. You just punched the ruler of Costa Luna."

Carter's jaw dropped in horror. "Oh, Rosie! I didn't mean—"

"Kidding! I couldn't resist," Rosie said, smiling. "It feels so good to be here. Of course, I love being home in Costa Luna with my mother and all my good friends at the palace. I've learned so much carrying out my royal duties. But when I am with you, I feel like a real, true teenager."

Just then Mr. Mason knocked on the door and came in pushing a wheeled cart containing two silver-domed platters. "Dinner, ladies? I took the liberty of doubling Carter's order, Rosie. I hope you like PB & J."

"Peanut butter and jelly," Carter translated when she saw Rosie's puzzled look.

Rosie's face lit up. "Oh, I haven't had a peanut butter and jelly sandwich since I was in Louisiana with you. Chef refused to make it for me back at the palace. He said it offended his taste buds."

Carter lifted one dome. Underneath was a delicious-looking sandwich, a glass bowl of carrot sticks with a container of ranch dressing, an icy cold strawberry smoothie, and a small bag of potato chips. Carter picked up the bag, crushed the contents, and opened it up. Then she lifted the top slice of bread from her sandwich and dumped the chips on top. "Strange? He hasn't seen nothin' yet."

"How did you know about this place?" Rosie asked as she and Carter paid for their admission tickets and headed inside the museum. Rosie had several official engagements during the day, but she had two free hours that morning.

"My dad told me," Carter said, shoving her change inside her pocket. "He said that of all the amazing museums D.C. has to offer, this one we could probably cover in just a couple of hours." She grinned. "And after all we've been through with the Princess Protection Program, it sounded perfect for us."

Instead of sculptures or paintings or Native American artifacts, this museum was dedicated to spies!

The place was so cool; there were tons of things to see and learn. And thankfully, Carter and Rosie were able to enjoy it without creating a mob scene.

Because Costa Luna was such a small country, Rosie was able to visit many public places in foreign countries without incident— she was rarely recognized. It had taken a little persuading, but Jorge and Victor had finally agreed to lag a little further behind the princess than usual, allowing the two girls to catch up in private.

If you looked at her, you'd never know she was a queen, Carter thought proudly. Good job, if I do say so myself. After all, she was the one responsible for teaching Rosie how to be a typical American teenager. Rosie wore a pair of ratty-looking sneakers, jeans, and a hoodie, with hardly any makeup; her hair was pulled back in a low ponytail.

After they watched a short film about real-life spies, the two friends toured an exhibit made up of hundreds of spy gadgets.

"This is amazing," Rosie said, reading a plaque about invisible ink.

Carter peered at a complicated-looking camera. "James Bond has nothing on these people." She wondered what, if any, of these kinds of gadgets her dad had used. She'd have to ask him about it later.

Anything and everything a person would ever want to know about espionage was here. "The life of a spy isn't a cakewalk," Carter said after they viewed some of the interactive exhibits.

Rosie nodded. "That is why it is best left to the professionals."

"But did you see that Queen Elizabeth I was a spy? Looks like you aren't the first royal to do some undercover snooping," Carter teased.

"Shhh," Rosie whispered, her eyes wide. "I'm trying to maintain my cover of typical American teen, remember?" She looked around quickly, hoping no one overheard. Then she turned back to Carter. "Come on, let's see what else is here."

They explored all the exhibits and galleries, and after grabbing a bite to eat, decided to end their visit with a quick trip to the museum gift shop.

Carter wanted to buy everything. There were cute T-shirts and hats and CDs and books—but best of all were the gadgets: special cameras, binoculars, and even night-vision goggles.

"Check out this thingamajig," Carter said, holding up a box. "It's a voice transformer."

Rosie motioned her over and pointed to a display of what looked like gift cards. "It's the ultimate room key!"

On the surface it was an average electronic key card. It even said WELCOME. But the back of the "key" slid off to reveal a tiny tool kit for picking a lock.

"They need one of these for cars, too." Carter wrinkled her nose. "Locking your keys in your car? Not fun." She reached into her pocket and pulled out a handful of crumpled dollar bills. "I'm going to get it. Who knows when I might need it?" she said, joking. She knew her dad would roll his eyes when he saw the tool kit. It probably wouldn't even work. And he hated to see her waste her hard-earned money. But it was cute and fun and would remind her of her trip to D.C. every time she saw it in her wallet.

Rosie picked up a copy of a book called

Spies Through the Years: Why We Love Them. "For when I get some downtime," she explained, handing it to the cashier. Then she linked her arm in Carter's. "This has been so much fun, but we better get going."

It was time for regular Rosie to transform into Queen Rosalinda. And it was time for Carter to hit the books and do some homework before the big dinner that night. Or maybe watch a good old-fashioned spy movie back at the hotel.

Chapter
3

*C*arter had to pinch herself over and over again as she and her father stepped out of the black limousine that night and walked down a flower-lined sidewalk that led to the White House.

This is unreal, Carter thought, trying to take everything in as they stopped at a security checkpoint. When they were cleared, they walked through a set of double doors and up a red-carpeted staircase. Along the staircase were portraits of past presidents. Carter recognized Richard Nixon and Woodrow Wilson. I remember when I did a paper in fourth grade on President Wilson, she thought, smiling to herself. If someone had told her then that one day she'd walk through the same halls he had, she never would have believed it.

"We're going to the East Room," her father whispered to her as they entered a large white room with a sky-high ceiling, heavy golden drapes, and ornate, cut-glass chandeliers.

"You know your house is big when you actually have names for the rooms," she whispered back.

"Can you imagine what our customers back at the Bait Shack would say if they could see us now?" her father asked. He squeezed her hand. He was clearly as excited as she was.

"They'd say you clean up real good," Carter said, kidding him. Seeing her dad in a tux—and not his usual cotton T-shirt, fishing vest, khakis, and wading boots—

took some getting used to. All the men were dressed in tuxes while the women wore ball gowns in a rainbow of colors, with shimmering jewels decorating their ears, wrists, and necklines.

Carter took a deep, steadying breath and grinned as a flute trio in the corner struck up a tune. Chances were she wouldn't be back at the White House anytime soon. She was going to enjoy each and every minute of it.

A waiter offered them each a glass of sparkling water. Taking a sip, Carter caught a glimpse of her reflection in the window. Wow, she thought. I guess I clean up real good, too.

Although she and Rosie couldn't get dressed together as they'd done before the homecoming dance, Rosie had arranged for Carter to get her hair and nails done at the hotel's salon. The stylist had done a great job. Her long dark hair fell in soft waves around her face. Lilac eye shadow had been swept across her lids, framing her black eyelashes. On her cheeks was the barest dusting of blush, and on her lips was a rosy pink gloss.

The best part was the dress that Mr. Elegante had sent over to the suite. It was a strapless pale lavender silk that fit Carter perfectly. Not too bad, she thought with a smile.

As her father made small talk with a couple, Carter looked around the room. Rosie had promised that there would be some famous faces there, and she wasn't kidding. Carter spotted the quarterback from last year's Super Bowl–winning team— he looked even more handsome in person. And was that Céline Dion? Carter took a sip of her water and tried to appear nonchalant. What if Céline came over to talk to her? Oh,

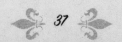

yes, the White House is charming, isn't it? Carter imagined herself saying. I mean, I'm just . . . charmed. I'm sure. Carter shook her head. She'd be better off staying away from the celebrities.

And then a hush fell over the room, and Carter snapped out of her thoughts. The First Lady had just entered the East Room! She warmly welcomed all the guests, and Carter overheard her telling several funny anecdotes. Then she invited everyone into the State Dining Room for the official dinner. "I wish we could take pictures," Carter whispered to her dad as they followed everyone down the corridor to the dining room. No cameras were allowed. Security had double-checked Carter's small clutch at the checkpoint.

"You could. But the year you'd have to spend in a cold, dark cell wouldn't really be worth it."

"Dad!" she said, elbowing him.

They picked up their place cards on a table outside the room. "We're not together," Carter said, frowning. "I'm at table eight and you're at table two. That's the First Lady's table, Dad!" It must have been because of all the incredible work her father had done over the past year for the Princess Protection Program. Even though it was a secret organization, the right people were made aware of its special accomplishments.

"All in a day's work," Mr. Mason joked. "Dining with the First Lady at the White House."

The room was filling up quickly with dinner guests, and Carter craned her neck, trying to see if she could spot Rosie.

"Maybe Rosie tried to have you seated next to a cute prince," her dad said with a wink.

Carter frowned. "*Daaaad*," she said. Talking about boys with her father was always weird.

Her dad gave her hand a squeeze and then headed off to find his seat. "See you later, pal."

"Later, Dad," Carter replied. Taking a deep breath, she made her way through the crowd toward her table. She'd counted fifteen tables in all, and hers was right in the middle of the room. An older man and woman were already there as well as an attractive young woman with white blond hair who was sitting across from the couple.

"Hello," Carter said politely when she arrived. A large candelabra decorated with white orchids sat in the middle of the table. She found her name written in script on a small card on the place setting next to the young woman. "I'm Carter Mason."

The older couple looked up at her. "I'm

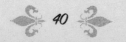

Fred Parker, and this is my wife, Marilyn," the man said. His wife smiled primly.

"Nice to meet you," Carter said and sat down. Maybe these were the wealthy donor types Rosie had mentioned.

"It's lovely to meet you, Carter," the young woman said, flashing a bright smile. "I am Alice Catherine, the—" She stopped as another young woman, also blond, joined them. She took the seat on the other side of Carter.

"And I am her cousin, Ingrid," said the woman, smoothing down her skirt.

"I can see the family resemblance," Carter told Ingrid.

"Really," Ingrid said, her tone flat. She smiled, but Carter got the sense that the comment annoyed her. That's weird, she thought. Alice Catherine was quite beautiful. She meant it as a compliment.

The two cousins looked just a few years

older than Carter. She guessed maybe nineteen. Alice Catherine's hair was pulled back in a tight bun and held by a jeweled pin with some sort of crest inside it. Ingrid's hair was cut in a short bob that showed off a pair of enormous sapphire earrings.

"We used to trick the servants at the castle all the time," Alice Catherine told Carter, laughing. "Remember, Ingrid? We were incorrigible. Simply dreadful!"

"Hmm," Ingrid said, nodding. "Bad beyond correction, Your Highness."

Carter blinked. Castle? Your Highness? Were these girls . . . princesses?

Of course! Rosie had mentioned Alice Catherine—HRH the crown princess of Scandia! And her cousin was a princess as well?

Carter felt even more nervous now, sitting in between two royal cousins. She knew she had to be on her best behavior. She couldn't do anything to embarrass

Rosie. Or Costa Luna. Or Louisiana!

Following Alice Catherine's lead, she picked up the folded white linen napkin that sat in front of her and draped it over her lap. On top of her gold-rimmed plate sat a small specially printed dinner menu on heavy cream-colored paper.

Fresh pea soup

❧

Sea scallops with mango chutney

❧

Medallions of beef tenderloin
Fricassee of baby vegetables
Buttermilk mashed potatoes
Roasted young carrots

❧

Bibb salad with green goddess dressing
Trio of farmhouse cheeses

❧

Mixed berry crumble
Tea and coffee service

Another man joined their table. "John Bolton," he said as he sat down. "I'm with the *Tribune*."

Everyone at the table introduced themselves again. After Carter told the reporter her name, he said, "Of?"

Carter looked at him blankly. Then responded, "Of what?"

"What country are you from?" Mr. Bolton asked slowly.

"This one," she replied, matching his tone. "I'm from Louisiana."

"Oh!" He laughed. "I thought you were a royal as well."

Carter felt a deep blush creeping up her neck and into her cheeks. "Nope. Just an ordinary girl." She took a sip of her water, relieved when the reporter turned his attention to the other adults.

"The last state dinner we were at was for the president of Mexico. It was extraordinary,

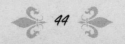

wasn't it, darling?" Mrs. Parker said to her husband.

"That's why we were so looking forward to this one," Mr. Parker told them. "It will be an evening to remember, for certain." Carter listened as the Parkers and Mr. Bolton debated the fascinating subject of state dinners. Then they moved on to vermeil candelabras, organic gardening, and the history of presidential china.

Carter looked over at Rosie's table. Her friend was laughing and smiling, and seemed utterly captivated by her dining partner, a portly woman wearing a magenta evening gown and a silly hat. Rosie is so good at being a queen, Carter marveled. Being royal is as natural to her as breathing. Rosie looked at Carter then and winked. Carter waved quickly before Rosie was swept back up into the conversation.

"I always look forward to dining at the

White House," Alice Catherine said as the waiter brought out the first course, pea soup. "It is like being with close friends."

Carter smiled as she picked up her soup spoon and dipped it into the steaming broth. She'd never had a five-course meal before—unless you counted hush puppies, onion rings, burgers, chocolate shakes, and brownies.

Probably not.

The state dinner was now in full swing—and so were the Strolling Strings—incredible musicians who were making their way around the ornate room. The president had offered a toast in honor of the king and queen of Pacardi, the two princes, HRH Princess Alice Catherine, and Queen Rosalinda of Costa Luna, welcoming everyone to the United States and to the White House. After the president's toast, the king had offered one of his own. Then the brothers gave long, uninspiring speeches. Alice Catherine made a sweet and charming statement, followed at last by Rosie, who said how honored she was to be here with the president and first lady, and wished everyone much happiness. There had been so much toasting that Carter had begun to wonder if they'd ever get to the third, fourth, and fifth courses of the meal.

But they had. And everything had been delicious. Now all that was left was dessert.

Keeping her phone out of sight under her napkin, Carter quickly typed a text to Rosalinda:

Baitgirl: ur tst was rlly good!!

She hesitated a moment before hitting SEND. Even if Rosie's phone was on, she really couldn't check her messages while

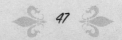

talking shop with the president and First Lady. Carter closed her phone. She would just have to remember to tell her friend how great her toast had been later.

Just then, Rosalinda looked up from her conversation and caught Carter's eye. She winked.

Carter put a big smile on her face. And then her shoulders slumped as she saw Rosie get caught up in yet another conversation.

Carter sighed. She was starting to get a little bored. She knew if her father saw her playing with her cell phone at the table, he'd give her his "Can't that wait?" look. It wasn't as if she was hurting anyone, though. She had even noticed Ingrid covertly texting someone. Ingrid had a cool phone—credit-card thin, with a bright purple skin and a tiara made out of crystals on it. Crystals? Probably diamonds.

"Would you excuse me?" Ingrid said,

startling her. The men at the table stood as Ingrid got up and walked toward the doorway. Carter watched her go, her posture perfect, her yellow skirt swishing. Ingrid had been polite enough, but there was something about her that seemed a little off. Maybe she's bored, too, Carter thought with a smile.

"Did you know there are thirty-five bathrooms here?" Carter said, turning to Alice Catherine. She'd done some reading up before the trip. She liked quirky facts the best.

"Well, then Ingrid has no excuse for taking too long," the princess replied, smiling. "Unless, of course, she does a little exploring. I've heard there are one-hundred thirty-two rooms here spread out over six levels. It's quite incredible."

"Is your, uh, castle this big?" Carter asked, hoping it wasn't a rude question.

The princess shook her head. "Oh, no. It's quite modest by royal standards. In fact, it's almost cozy. I like it that way. I think I'd get lost here!"

She seems so down-to-earth, Carter thought. Kind of like Rosie. If you replaced her evening gown and fancy jewels with a T-shirt and a pair of jeans, she could pass for a college student.

"So, what brings you to this dinner, Carter?" Alice Catherine asked pleasantly.

"Oh, I'm a good friend of Rosie— I mean, Queen Rosalinda's," Carter replied. "Are you going to be queen one day, too?"

Alice Catherine nodded. "Yes, soon. But just like in Costa Luna, my country has gone through some changes." She paused, then finally continued, "You see, years ago, the reigning king or queen's first-born *son* was heir to the throne. Then, a constitutional reform took place, changing the way succession worked. Now, the throne is inherited by the monarch's eldest child—boy *or* girl."

"And that's you?" Carter asked.

"Yes." Alice Catherine sighed. "But I have a younger brother, Peter, who is now no longer heir to the throne. This was very upsetting to my father, as he had great dreams for when Peter became king."

"Well, I'm sure you'll be a fantastic queen," Carter said impulsively. "And you shouldn't feel guilty. I mean, it's not your fault that they changed the law."

Alice Catherine nodded again. "I know. And even if something were to happen to me, Peter still wouldn't be king. The new law says that the throne would then pass to my father's brother's eldest child—Ingrid."

"Hello. I heard my name." Surprised, Carter turned to see that Ingrid had already returned. There was a fresh coat of gloss on her lips. Mr. Parker and John Bolton stood as Ingrid took her seat.

"I was just telling Carter about our country," Alice Catherine said.

"Oh," Ingrid said. "Have you ever been to Scandia, Carter?"

"No." Carter shrugged. "I've never really been anywhere besides Louisiana. And Costa Luna. And now here."

Alice Catherine smiled kindly as Ingrid shrugged.

Carter felt her cheeks growing warm. She'd never felt embarrassed by her lack of worldly knowledge before. But then again, she'd never dined with the crown princess of a foreign country and her successor before.

Carter tucked her cell into her purse and jumped up from her chair. There had never been a more perfect moment for a quick trip to the bathroom.

"Be right back," she whispered to Alice Catherine. Then she scurried for the door.

A waiter pointed her in the direction of the ladies' room. As she walked down the corridor, she peered curiously into the rooms she passed. It would be so cool to check out a few of those 132 rooms. Maybe she could just pop into one. . . .

"Miss?" a woman in a black suit with an earpiece said, jolting her from her thoughts. "The ladies' room is through this door."

"Oh. Um, thanks," Carter said. It would be more fun to explore with Rosie, anyway. And Rosie wouldn't have to sneak. She could probably get them a guided tour.

Carter was drying her hands and getting ready to walk out of the bathroom when she spotted a purple cell phone on the vanity. Curious, she picked it up and looked around for a ladies' room attendant or a lost-and-found basket. Not finding either one, she decided to turn it in to the guard who had directed her to the bathroom. She would know the protocol for lost items at state dinners. Carter was just about to walk out the door when she turned the phone in her hand and saw a tiny crystal tiara. It was Ingrid's! "She must have left it here by mistake," Carter said. "I'll bring it back to her. Maybe that will trigger her nice gene." Suddenly, the phone began to vibrate. An envelope popped up on the display, signaling a new text.

"Cool," Carter said as she watched the envelope circle the screen. She'd have to tell her dad that when it was time for an upgrade, this was the model to buy.

As Carter was walking back down the hall to the dining room, the phone vibrated again, and this time it beeped long and loud. Startled, Carter hit the volume button on the side. She looked around the near-empty corridor. No one seemed to notice she was even there. She breathed a sigh of relief. She didn't want to get in trouble for a loud phone that wasn't even hers!

Carter looked down at the display. She froze. The text message was open, and she couldn't believe what it said:

Lapofluxury: r u thr? dont tell me u r chickening out. u promised u wld do this 4 me. 4 us. gtng AC out of the pic is the only way.

Chapter 4

Carter's heart was thumping faster than a racehorse's. She stared down at the cell phone in her hand as if it were a poisonous hot potato.

Chickening out? Getting AC out of the picture?

Carter shook her head. It was none of her business. And it probably didn't mean what she thought it meant. AC could stand for anything—air conditioning, advanced calculus. . . .

But in her heart she knew that wasn't true. She was ninety-eight percent sure that AC stood for Alice Catherine. And it sounded like Ingrid was wrapped up in some sort of plot to hurt her.

I knew there was something weird about her, Carter thought, her full stomach lurching. Alice Catherine seemed so good-natured. Why would anyone want to do her harm?

The crown princess's words came flooding back to Carter's brain. *If something were to happen to me, Peter still wouldn't be king. The throne would then pass to my father's brother's eldest child—Ingrid.*

Carter knew how dangerous being a princess could be. Her father had gone on a number of serious missions. And probably some that were even more dangerous that she didn't even know about. She had to tell him what was going on, and fast. It could be a matter of life or death for Alice Catherine.

The phone vibrated again, and Carter let out a small shriek. She took a deep breath.

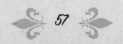

She needed to get back to the dinner, tell her father what she suspected, and then eat her dessert, never letting Alice Catherine out of her sight.

Just as she reached for the handle, the door swung open. Carter's heart sank. It was Ingrid. And she seemed frantic.

"Oh, thank goodness! You found my cell," she said. Her blue eyes examined Carter carefully as she held out her hand for the phone.

"Yes. Yes, I did," Carter said, quickly handing it over. "You, uh, left it on the vanity in the bathroom. I saw you using it earlier and so I knew it was yours. I, um, was just bringing it back to you, Your Highness."

Smooth, Carter thought. She willed herself to remain calm, cool, and collected.

"How kind of you," Ingrid said, sliding the phone into her purse. Her eyes searched Carter's face.

As soon as Ingrid checked her phone, would she see that Carter had read the text? Carter did not want to be around for that.

Before Ingrid could say another word, Carter pointed through the open doors. "I see Rosalinda looking for me," she said. She waved at her friend, who was, thankfully, looking in her direction. Rosie waved back just as Ingrid turned to look.

Carter smiled and then hurried into the room.

"Are you having a good time?" Rosie asked when Carter approached her. "Alice Catherine is very kind, isn't she?"

"Yes, I am," Carter said. "And she is. Hey, have you seen my dad?"

"Sorry, I haven't, Carter," Rosie answered. Then she perked up. "Oh, the president wants us for photos now. I'll see you later."

Carter looked over at her father's table; he wasn't there.

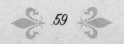

She walked slowly back to her table wondering where her father was. Her head swiveled, trying to find him in the busy, buzzing room.

Dad, where are you? she thought desperately.

The Parkers and Mr. Bolton were drinking their coffee when Carter sat down at the table.

"A man left that for you," Mr. Parker said, indicating Carter's plate. A folded note sat on top of it.

Her mouth dry, Carter picked up the note and read.

Carter—something has come up. If you need to reach me, Jorge and Victor can contact the Program headquarters and they'll send me a message. They'll be watching out for you while I'm away. Don't worry, I'll be back in two days, max. Charge whatever you need

to the room. Enjoy D.C. with Rosie. I'm sorry
I couldn't say good-bye.
Love you!
   Dad

   Great. This was just great. Why did her
father have to be called off on an emergency
mission now?

   Carter was really close to her dad. She
didn't like when he left her. But this time she
disliked it even more than usual. Not only
didn't she have the chance to tell him to be
careful, or to do their traditional good-bye
fist bump, she also didn't have the chance to
tell him that a real, live princess emergency
was going down right around her. Smack in
the middle of the White House.

Chapter
5

Carter was sure that the mixed-berry crumble was probably delicious—after all, it had been made by the White House dessert chef. But right now it tasted like cardboard in her mouth. She couldn't stop thinking about the text message. And where on Earth was her dad?

She caught Mrs. Parker's eye and managed a weak smile. Then she picked up her teacup and downed its contents in one big gulp. Her father had told her over and over again that she was under no circumstances to get involved with anything dangerous. "Missions are for the professionals, Carter," she could hear him saying to her, almost as if he were there by her side.

Under normal circumstances, she would listen to her dad's advice. She knew that she could go to Jorge and Victor. In fact, that's what her dad told her to do. But for some reason, she felt that she had to figure out what was really going on before she dragged Rosie's personal security detail into the mix.

Besides, she told herself, wiping her mouth with her napkin, maybe it's all a misunderstanding. If she could talk to Alice Catherine about Ingrid, maybe she'd discover that the cousins were the best of friends.

People were milling around now, chatting about how nice the evening had been so far, and about how much they were looking forward to the after-dinner entertainment. There were going to be a cellist and concert pianist in the East Room.

Carter wondered if she'd have a chance

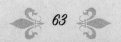

to talk to Rosie before the concert began. She might have an idea about what to do. But Rosie was in the middle of a massive photo session with ambassadors, senators, and other visiting dignitaries. Her beautiful smile never left her face.

Rosie wasn't going to be free from her royal duties anytime soon. Carter tried to catch Rosie's eye—frantic eyebrow-raising, a wave—but Rosie just didn't look her way.

When the pianist had finished playing his final, thrilling piece, the audience rose to their feet, bursting with applause. But Carter was too lost in her own thoughts to move. The text on Ingrid's phone had made it sound as if whatever was going to happen was going to happen very soon. Like, maybe, even tonight. What if there was some sort of assassination attempt on Alice Catherine's life right here, right now? Her father was the one sworn to protect princesses, not her. But she wouldn't be able to forgive herself if anything happened.

Carter decided that if she couldn't get Rosie's input, she'd have to do the next best thing—stick to Alice Catherine's side like glue. The crown princess had stopped to chat to a cluster of admirers. Then she had retrieved her wrap from the coat-check room and thanked the musicians for playing such beautiful music.

And Carter was there for every minute of it. Unfortunately, someone else was also sticking to Alice Catherine's side. Ingrid.

"It was so nice to get to meet you," Carter told the princesses as they stood in the crush of people waiting to leave the White House. She sent Rosie a text:

Baitgirl: i no u r real busy but call me as soon as u can!!!!

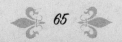

"And you as well," Alice Catherine said graciously.

"Yes," Ingrid said, her arms folded tightly across her chest.

"Are you guys taking a taxi back to your hotel?" Carter asked.

Ingrid looked at her as if she had three heads. "No."

"We have a car waiting for us," Alice Catherine explained. "We're actually going to visit an old family friend now."

Carter was wondering how they'd know which car was theirs since there seemed to be a gazillion black cars lined up outside waiting for guests. Then a flurry of lights started going off.

"Stupid media," Ingrid muttered under her breath as a reporter called out Alice Catherine's name.

"There she is! Your Highness! Over here! Over here! How was the dinner? How long will you be in the U.S.?"

For a moment, Carter took her eyes off the princess, blinking as flashes popped around her. Everyone seemed to want a part of Alice Catherine—a word, a smile, a wave, a photo. And that was when Carter felt a push as she stepped off the curb.

"Noooo," Carter shrieked as she stumbled forward, clutching at the air. Thankfully, she caught her balance in time.

But her purse wasn't so lucky. Carter watched in dismay as it sailed ahead of her— and under the tire of a long, black limousine pulling out onto the road. *Crunch!* Carter groaned.

"Here you are, miss," a uniformed guard said when he handed Carter her smashed-up clutch. "You should be more careful with your belongings."

"Yeah. Thanks." The purse was basically useless now. The clasp was broken, and there were large tread marks running over the fabric. She found her room key still intact, but the wand was now sticking out of her cracked lip gloss tube as pink lip gloss dripped out.

Her pretty silver cell phone was mangled and mashed. If Rosie tried to call or text her now, Carter would be out of luck.

"Oh, Carter! Are you all right? Your purse," Alice Catherine said, her voice filled with concern.

"Bad luck," Ingrid said, slowly shaking her head.

Carter couldn't help but look at Ingrid through cold eyes. *Someone* had pushed her. And Ingrid was standing in the perfect spot. . . .

She clutched her ruined purse and turned her attention to trying to remember what her car and driver looked like. Then she felt a hand gently touch her arm.

"That never would have happened if you hadn't been with us," Alice Catherine said, shaking her head. "Reporters sometimes get a little zealous in their pursuit of a shot. It's crazy, really."

Carter was about to say that she didn't think a reporter was responsible for her stumble off the curb. But before she could say a word, the crown princess said something that made Carter forget all about her lost gum and ruined lip gloss—and almost, but not quite, her ruined cell.

"Let us make it up to you," Alice Catherine said impulsively. "I have a number of official duties while here in Washington, and it would be an honor if you could accompany us on a few of them tomorrow." She hesitated. "Unless you have prior commitments with Queen Rosalinda?"

Carter promptly shook her head. What an incredible stroke of luck. Now she would be able to keep an eye on the princess while she was waiting to talk to her father. "Nope! Because this is Rosie—I mean, Rosalinda's—first visit to the U.S. as queen, she has tons of extremely important meetings tomorrow at the State Department. We won't be able to get together until dinner."

Alice Catherine grinned. "Well, you see, I'm practically an old hat at this. I've been to the United States with my parents many times. I'm so thrilled you'll be joining us tomorrow." She turned to her cousin. "Right, Ingrid? It's the least we can do."

"Hmm, yes," Ingrid replied, as a man in a dark suit opened the door of the limousine that had pulled up in front of them. "No problem at all."

It was pretty obvious to Carter that Ingrid was not happy with this news. But I can't worry about that, Carter thought. The crown princess had invited her, after all, not Ingrid. And staying close to her was the only way she could think of to keep her safe.

"Fantastic!" Alice Catherine said as she followed her cousin into the waiting car and then put the window down. "So we'll meet you at the hotel concierge's desk tomorrow morning," she called out, leaning on the windowsill. "Eightish?"

Carter nodded. "I'll be ready." She held up her hand and waved as the limo pulled off into the night. She shivered in her lavender dress, wishing she could blink herself back to her hotel room and be all wrapped up in one of those bathrobes under the down comforter.

I'll be alone, she remembered, letting out a sigh. But there was no time for a pity party. This was a time for action. She'd be totally okay. She'd stayed home at the cabin plenty of times when her father had to go off on a mission. Being in D.C. wouldn't be any different. Except for Jorge and Victor being just a phone call away and the higher thread count on her sheets.

Carter made a mental list of the advantages of being in a fancy hotel suite by herself:

> *I can stay up as late as I want.*
> *No waiting to use the shower.*
> *I can leave the cap off the toothpaste.*
> *I can jump on the bed and no one will*
> *know (except maybe the people in the*
> *room below mine).*

Just then Carter spotted her driver, Mike—or rather, he spotted her. He pulled up, and she climbed gratefully into the car. "Your father had to leave early," Mike told her—a statement, not a question.

Carter nodded, kicking off her shoes.

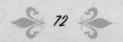

"Yep, I know. Just me now." And that made her think of one more item for her list. "Would you mind stopping at the pizza place a few blocks from the hotel?" she asked hopefully, raising an eyebrow. As Mike obliged with a tip of his hat, she relaxed back into the soft leather seat. She'd end this roller-coaster day with a slice of pepperoni pizza in a huge fluffy bed, and maybe some candy from the goodies cabinet. Then she'd plan her next move.

The princess's safety depended on it.

Chapter 6

"The children are incredibly excited about meeting you, Your Highness," the principal said as she led the group down the corridor, her heels clicking on the polished floor tiles. Carter, Alice Catherine, Ingrid, two security guards, each of the princesses' assistants, two journalists, and a photographer were at the Harney Elementary School. Alice Catherine's first official engagement of the day was reading a picture book to a group of kids.

Principal Joanne was smiling broadly, but Carter could tell she was slightly nervous by the way she played with the buttons on her jacket. This was probably the first royal person ever to stroll down the hallway of Harney Elementary. The curious faces of kids, teachers, and janitors peeked out from classrooms and doorways, trying to catch a glimpse of the princesses.

Carter was nervous, too—but not for the same reason. She was afraid that something was going to happen to the princess. Without her cell phone, there had been no way for her to call Rosie. The only place she'd stored Rosie's number was in her phone's speed dial—number two, just after her dad. Jorge and Victor had come by Carter's room that morning to give her Rosalinda's schedule for the day and the times Carter was expected to check in with them. She was just about to mention her ruined cell when Victor's phone beeped and the two men rushed off.

I hope Rosie doesn't think I'm blowing

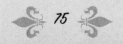

her off, Carter thought, sighing. She hated when people got the wrong impression about something.

Carter had woken up, showered with the cute little White House soap, then put on her black jeans and tan sweater. When she'd opened her hotel-room door to go downstairs to grab a bagel in the lobby, she'd found a copy of the day's newspaper folded outside her door.

Cool, she thought, planning to do the crossword puzzle until she saw the page featuring photos from last night's state dinner. There was Rosie, sandwiched in between the president and first lady, a regal smile on her face. And there were the two princes, Nicholas and Pavlos, posing with some senators, and a shot of Ingrid schmoozing with the king and queen of Pacardi.

But the photo they showed of Alice Catherine? It was taken seconds after Carter tripped. The crown princess had a goofy look on her face, her arms outstretched. Carter knew it was because the princess was trying to save her from falling. But the caption read: A ROYAL KLUTZ?

That was kind of mean, Carter thought, crumpling the paper up.

But the princess didn't seem to be bothered at all. I guess that kind of thing happens to famous people a lot, Carter decided. Alice Catherine had chatted pleasantly throughout the car ride to the school. She seemed truly interested in learning all about the student body, the neighborhood, and the issues that were important to Principal Joanne and how she could help. Carter, meanwhile, had kept her eye on Ingrid the whole time. Nothing strange had happened since the previous night. But Carter was still uneasy . . . and the way Ingrid kept looking at her . . .

"Here we are," the principal said, interrupting Carter's thoughts. The group had stopped outside a classroom door. "Mrs. Martin's first-grade class." When the door opened and the group walked in, Carter smiled. Brightly colored math and spelling posters lined the walls. A low row of hooks held coats and backpacks. And everywhere was adorable artwork the children had made for the princesses.

There were Scandian flags made out of construction paper and little castle replicas made from popsicle sticks and graham crackers. But Carter's favorites were the crayon portraits of Alice Catherine and Ingrid, complete with tiaras.

The class of about twenty-five children, wearing their very best clothes, stood up from their pint-size desks and curtsied or bowed.

"Good morning, Your Highnesses," they said to Alice Catherine and Ingrid.

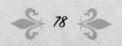

"Good morning," the princesses replied.

"We're so happy to—*achoo*!—be with you today," Alice Catherine told them as Ingrid nodded.

The teacher spoke for a few minutes, telling them about all the preparations that had been made for their visit. Then a little girl walked up and handed the princesses a bouquet of pretty flowers.

"All right, class," Mrs. Martin announced. "Let's take our places on the rug." The children sat down on a bright orange carpet while Alice Catherine took the seat the teacher indicated—a rocking chair covered with a quilt that read: READING IS COOL!

Not quite a throne, but a lot more comfy, Carter thought, as she took a seat on one of the little kid chairs. Ingrid stood near the back of the room with the assistants and journalists; the security guards were posted at the door.

For the first time that morning, Carter allowed herself to relax. She knew that Alice Catherine's security detail had already visited the school to make sure all necessary security measures were in place. Nothing was going to happen to the princess at Harney Elementary School.

Unless you counted a severe case of the sneezes. Alice Catherine had barely begun to read when she sneezed again. And . . . again. "'And then Charlie told the big bad troll that there was no'—*achoo!*—'way that he was going to frighten him'—*achoo!*—'anymore.'" A few of the children giggled.

"Do you have a cold?" a boy asked.

The princess was doing everything in her power to not let the sneezing stop her. She tried to smile as she pinched the tip of her nose. She asked for a drink of water. She rubbed her eyes. She cleared her throat. But nothing helped. "I don't know why—

achoo!—this is happening!" she whispered apologetically to the students.

It's like the time Donny put pepper in Eddie Jones's gym bag, making sure it coated his uniform, Carter thought. Poor Eddie sneezed through an entire basketball game.

Pepper! That was it. Carter had been waiting for something to happen. She'd expected something like Ingrid suddenly tackling Alice Catherine or someone bursting into the room to kidnap her. But it looked as if she was dealing with a much sneakier, more subtle opponent.

Because now Alice Catherine was excusing herself to go to the ladies' room with her assistant and one of the agents . . . and Ingrid had smoothly stepped forward to take her place in the rocking chair. "Let's keep reading while the princess gets herself sorted out," Ingrid cooed in a sickly sweet voice. "I can't wait to find out what happens!"

Carter watched as Ingrid picked up the picture book and began to read. "'The troll was very, very angry,'" Ingrid read, her eyes wide. "'In fact, he was so angry he took Charlie deep underground and locked him up where no one would ever find him.'"

The kids were hanging on her every word. Carter narrowed her eyes. What a perfect story for Ingrid to read, Carter thought as she listened.

Sure, no real harm had come to Alice Catherine just yet. But, Carter worried, if the princess started the day off with a sneeze-fest . . . how would she end it?

Finally, Alice Catherine returned to the room with her sneezing under control—but not before Ingrid had stolen the show with her animated reading of *three* picture books instead of just the one Alice Catherine had chosen. She'd posed for pictures with all of the children and had even participated in a class play. In short, she was a total hit with the kids at Harney Elementary School.

"That has never, ever, happened to me in my life," Alice Catherine was saying, her voice full of remorse as they exited the hospital where the princess had visited a number of patients on her second stop of the day. She'd sat with them, holding their hands and listening to their stories for two hours. Carter had found it really touching. That was what being a princess was all about. Using your celebrity to reach out and help those who were less fortunate than you were.

Thankfully, nothing crazy had gone on during the hospital visit.

Unfortunately Carter couldn't say the same thing about their third stop.

Everyone—the princesses, assistants, journalists, photographer, and security guards were at a huge ballpark where they were the special guests of honor at a minor-league baseball game. The princesses had changed into zip-front hoodies and matching baseball caps, both with the home team's logo. A flashing message board welcoming the princesses blinked continuously. By the way they hooted and cheered from the bleachers as the group made its way into the stands, it seemed that the entire crowd had been waiting for the royals to arrive.

Carter tried to blend into the background as the princesses and their entourage took their seats two rows behind home plate. After all, she was a total nobody to these people. She was on a mission, she reminded herself. A mission to get to the bottom of that text message.

But she also was kind of looking forward to the game. She and her dad loved watching baseball together. They had even gone to a college game once at Louisiana State

University. Carter had loved it—the sound of the bat meeting the ball, the dust cloud slides into the bases, the roar of the fans. Not to mention the funnel cakes, the chili cheese dogs, the caramel popcorn. They had seen a ninth-inning home run that sent the crowd into a frenzy.

Two eager-looking park employees brought everyone lemonade, hot dogs, and snacks. The first inning was under way. The home team was at bat, and the hitter had just struck out. Alice Catherine was seated on Carter's right and a journalist was on her left, his digital recorder in one hand, a soft pretzel in the other.

Carter was just taking a bite of her hot dog—mmm, ballpark perfect with spicy brown mustard and grilled to perfection—when, to her surprise, Alice Catherine stood up and yelled, "You're not as bad as I thought you'd be. You're worse!"

She sat down, grinning. Startled, Carter swallowed, wondering what had gotten into the princess. It seemed more than a little impolite.

And by the time they'd reached the fourth inning, her behavior had gone from bad to worse. Really worse.

"In the dictionary under *boring*, your team photo is there!" she had yelled out in the second inning.

"How old are you, first baseman?" she had shouted when he dropped the ball. Even more bizarre was that the crown princess seemed genuinely excited and pleased with herself. It's as if she thinks this is the way people act at a ball game, Carter thought. Except she's making fun of the home team! And, they're showing her on the Jumbo Tron!

The journalist next to Carter was gaping at Alice Catherine as if she had lost her mind. Maybe she has, Carter thought, quickly glancing over her shoulder at Ingrid. Someone had definitely put pepper or some kind of sneezing powder into something the princess had come into contact with at the school that morning. Did they put some kind of weird turn-me-rude dust in her lemonade? Ingrid was making a big show of looking completely horrified.

Carter couldn't stand it any longer. And by the dirty looks from the people sitting nearby, neither could the hometown fans. "Excuse me, Your Highness, but why do you keep insulting the players?" Carter whispered.

Alice Catherine smiled back at her, looking extrahappy with herself. "Well, thankfully someone left me a folder on sports protocol back at the hotel," she confided under her breath. "Otherwise, I would *never* have known that insulting the home team is the best compliment you can give." She took a big gulp of lemonade. "Am I being mean enough?"

Carter blinked in the afternoon sunlight, not sure what to say. Before she could figure out how to tell the princess that her behavior was not complimentary but that it was majorly rude, Alice Catherine added, "And believe me, Carter, after this morning's fiasco at Harney Elementary School, I want everything to go absolutely perfectly. And if telling the pitcher he stinks will show the American people how much I truly value being here, well, I say, play ball, losers!" She put her fingers between her teeth and whistled.

Carter was certain that Ingrid was the "helpful" person who had left the folder. But how could she prove it?

And, she thought uncomfortably, how far will Ingrid actually go?

Chapter 7

*C*arter was like a crazy person by the time she got back to the hotel. There was no doubt in her mind that Ingrid had it in for the princess. She was trying to make her look terrible, and she was succeeding. Carter had finally gotten Alice Catherine to quiet down at the ballpark. She hadn't really wanted to be the one to tell her the truth about how rude she was being, but if she hadn't, the princess never would have stopped. The royal entourage would probably have been booed out of the stadium.

Carter felt completely lost without her cell phone. She wasn't a person who had it stuck to her ear all the time, but not being able to communicate with her dad or Rosie was really getting to her.

When she got back to the hotel, Rosie had left a message for her at the front desk.

Carter,
    My meeting at the State Department was pushed back and I am unable to make dinner. I'm so sorry! We've barely seen each other. I will meet you at the reception tonight and we'll catch up then.
XO,
Rosie
P.S. Why haven't you answered your phone? Are you all right?

Carter sighed. Her first order of business at the cocktail reception was to tell

Rosie about her damaged phone. Then she'd tell her about everything else.

The cocktail reception was being held for the visiting dignitaries, and Carter got ready in record time. She wore the dress Mr. Elegante had sent her for the homecoming dance—but instead of heels she wore a pair of comfy flats. She wanted to be prepared in case she had to tackle an assassin or run after a bad guy . . . or girl.

She really wished her dad would get back! But at least tonight she'd have the chance to talk to Rosie and fill her in on what was going on. And if things got really bad, she promised herself she'd go straight to Jorge and Victor for help.

She took the elevator to the fourth floor and headed for the Crystal Ballroom, where the reception was being held. After passing the security check at the front door, she breezed into the cavernous space.

She spotted Rosie engaged in a discussion with a man in a military uniform. Where is Alice Catherine? she wondered, her eyes scanning the room. Carter checked her watch. The princess should definitely be here by now. She was about to hurry over to Rosie when she caught sight of Ingrid.

The princess was standing by a punch bowl speaking with a man carrying a mini–voice recorder and listening to Ingrid intently. She was wearing an elegant black gown, and her hair was swept back behind her ears.

Carter crept forward, positioning herself behind a giant potted fern.

"Sometimes she just doesn't show up," Ingrid was saying, her voice low and resigned. "Believe me, we all try our best, but she just can't seem to get anywhere on time."

The reporter was nodding. "I've heard that," he said knowingly.

Ingrid sighed. "You have no idea. She needs an entire team to get ready. If our countrymen knew that their hard-earned tax dollars were going to pay for a hairdresser, a makeup artist, a stylist, a color advisor, a personal assistant, and even a psychic, why—" Then she put a hand to her mouth. "You won't print that, right?"

Carter was furious. Color advisor? Psychic? Alice Catherine was about as low maintenance as a princess could be. She seemed exactly like Rosie—self-assured, honest, and smart. The type of person who would rather read to a child or hold a sick person's hand than attend a glitzy party or shop in a fancy store. The kind of princess Carter hadn't realized existed—and now admired wholeheartedly.

There was no doubt left in Carter's mind as to what was going on. Ingrid was trying to disgrace Alice Catherine on this important royal visit. All so she could claim the throne!

And she's not working alone, Carter reminded herself. She was so angry she almost burst through the plant leaves.

But that wouldn't be smart. And she had to be smart. Smart would save the day. It was just her luck that Rosie caught her eye, a questioning look on her face. Carter hesitated. She felt torn—she wanted to go and tell Rosie everything, but there just wasn't enough time.

"I can't talk now!" she mouthed, holding up her finger in a be-right-back gesture. And then she darted off, heading back to the elevator bank and up to the princess's floor. She got off at the eleventh floor, where she'd found out the Scandian princesses were staying. She glanced up and down the brightly lit hall. Good. No security detail. That made sense—the princesses were expected to be at the ball, so no guards were left manning their posts on this floor.

Carter tiptoed down the Persian-carpeted corridor until she reached room 1155—the crown princess's room. She felt a little bit like a detective in a mystery novel. And she felt even more like one when she reached into her purse and pulled out the key-card lock pick that she had purchased at the spy museum. Taking a deep breath, Carter slid off the back part of the card. Underneath were picks and a flat tension tool.

Okay. Let's see if this toy even works, she thought, her hands shaking slightly as she used one of the picks, and then another. She fumbled with the lock. In just a few minutes—bingo! The lock clicked open, and she pushed the door ajar and stepped over the threshold.

The suite had the same layout as Carter's, and she quickly looked in all the potential places the princess could be. Nothing. Carter walked over to the leaded glass door and swept the curtains aside. Alice Catherine was trapped outside on the balcony!

"Alice Catherine!" Carter cried. The princess was shivering in a thin silk dress, her arms wrapped around her slender frame.

"Carter! Thank goodness you're here," she said, her words somewhat muffled because of the glass. "Please. Help me!"

Carter tried to slide the door open, but it was jammed in place. "I—I can't get it!" Carter shouted. "Wait right here," she told her, realizing how ridiculous that sounded the moment the words were out of her mouth.

She ran out of the suite and down the hall to the stairwell. Her room was 1255—directly above the princess's. She hurried into her room, making sure the door closed firmly behind her. She tore the comforter from the bed and yanked off the sheets, tying the flat one to the fitted one. She did the same with the bedsheets in her father's room, and then tied all four sheets together, making one long makeshift rope.

I hope high thread count means these sheets will be strong enough to hold my weight, Carter thought nervously. She tied one end of the sheets to the most secure thing in the room—the bed leg—and then pushed through her own door onto the balcony. She looked down at Alice Catherine.

"Your Highness! Up here!" she called. She dropped the rope down and watched as Alice Catherine grabbed hold and pulled herself up foot by foot. "Don't look down," Carter added, pressing her eyes shut. If anything went wrong . . .

But it didn't. A few minutes later, Alice Catherine was standing inside Carter's suite, taking big deep breaths.

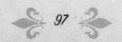

"Please. Sit down. Do you want some . . . cashews?" Carter asked. She poured some bottled water into a glass.

The princess sat on the edge of the unmade bed and shook her head. She drank the water in one big gulp.

"How in the world did you end up locked out on the balcony?" Carter asked.

The princess looked bewildered. "It was the strangest thing. I was in the bathroom brushing my teeth. When I came out, the door was open. I went to shut it, but something on the balcony caught my eye. There was a box wrapped with a silver bow. I walked out to pick it up, and suddenly the door slammed shut behind me."

"Did you see who it was?" Carter asked breathlessly.

The princess shook her head. "No. The drapes fell closed." Her forehead creased with worry. "But I must tell my security detail. This . . . this worries me, Carter." She let out a deep sigh. "I suppose the wind could have blown the door shut—or maybe it was housekeeping performing their nightly service, but the package . . ."

"Your Highness?" Carter paused. She knew what she was about to say would sound a little—okay, a lot—crazy. But she knew it was time to tell someone. And who better to tell than the person in danger? "I think your cousin is behind this. I think that she wants to take the throne. And that you are in grave danger."

Alice Catherine gasped. "What are you saying?"

Carter sat down next to her on the bed. "Look. I know I don't know you well. But trust me when I say I do know a thing or two about princesses in trouble."

The princess looked at her expectantly.

Carter hadn't expected Alice Catherine

to believe her every word. But she hadn't expected Alice Catherine to be so dismissive of the idea. It wasn't like Ingrid was kind or sweet or personable, at least as far as Carter had seen, "I'm saying that from the moment I met you both, I felt that there was something—I don't know—weird, about Ingrid," Carter continued. And then she told the princess about the text message.

But to her dismay, Alice Catherine still wasn't buying it. "Loyalty means everything to me, Carter. You do not understand. I grew up with Ingrid. We went to preschool together. We have shared many things over the years."

"Okay," Carter said, carefully choosing her words. "But I think things have changed, Your Highness. I've noticed how Ingrid always has to take a backseat when you're around. Maybe she's tired of it. The sneezing, the sports insults—it's all adding up to something rotten in my book."

Alice Catherine stood and began to pace back and forth. "Ingrid may not be . . . the kindest person, Carter. But she never had to learn to be front and center, to please everyone, like I did. And I know that it must be hard, at times, to be in my shadow. She has never complained, though. She has never made even the slightest protest. And I include her whenever I can. She is always a part of my joys and achievements. And I share what I have as next in line to the throne with her. She is like my sister, Carter."

"But I heard her, Your Highness," Carter protested, feeling her cheeks flush. "Tonight. At the reception. She was telling a reporter how you take forever to get dressed and—"

Alice Catherine held up her hand to silence her. "Stop. Please. I do not want to hear what you have to say. Ingrid would never hurt me." And with tears filling her eyes, she straightened her tiara and walked angrily out of the room.

Biting her lip, Carter hurried after her, not sure what to do. She managed to slip inside the elevator just before the doors closed. Awkward silence filled the tiny space as Alice Catherine stared straight ahead, wiping her eyes.

When they got to the fourth floor, Alice Catherine strode toward the ballroom, Carter right on her heels.

The reception was long since over. The musicians were gone. Workers were breaking down the tables, clearing the soiled linens and vacuuming the floor. Trays of dirty glasses and cocktail plates sat on catering trays waiting to be carted back to the kitchen.

A group of reporters were packing up their things in the corner, getting ready to

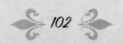

head out, when one of them turned and saw Alice Catherine and Carter standing in the doorway.

"Hey. There she is—the missing princess! Hey princess, you need a watch?"

And as they whipped out their cameras and began to take pictures of the flustered, upset princess, Carter realized that although the reception was over, the uproar about Alice Catherine's odd behavior was just about to begin.

Chapter 8

"I'm telling you. The girl is evil. Pure evil," Carter said firmly, crunching her wheat toast. At last, she and Rosie were together. It had taken a pitcher of freshly-squeezed orange juice, scrambled eggs, toast, extra-crispy bacon, and a round of hot chocolate to tell Rosie everything that had happened in the past two days. And it felt good to get it off her chest.

Rosie took a dainty bite of bacon. She had to make an appearance at ten, but for now she was happily incognito in her jeans and gray polo. They were in a private corner of the hotel dining room. No one was nearby except for Jorge and Victor who were two tables away, happily digging into their banana-nut pancakes.

"I agree, Carter. It strongly appears that Princess Ingrid is up to no good," Rosie told her. "And that is why we must contact the Director at the Princess Protection Program. With your father away, she is the only one who can tell us what to do."

"No, Rosie. We can't call her," Carter said, shaking her head. Carter didn't need the Director trying to figure out who was behind everything—Carter already knew. She was afraid that bringing program agents into the mix could slow everything down, and Carter knew that there was no time to waste.

Rosie hesitated. "But Carter. Remember homecoming?"

"How could I forget?" Carter smiled. "I helped bring an evil dictator to justice."

"Yes . . . and your father was furious that you hadn't gone to him first." Rosie looked troubled. "You were lucky, Carter. Your father showed up just in time. But now?" She twisted a strand of her long dark hair. "If anything goes wrong . . . you're on your own."

"I know." Carter stared down at her plate. "But what can I say? I found out that I love helping people. And if anyone needs help, it's Alice Catherine. But she refuses to believe me about what's going on." She let out a resigned sigh. "Look. As soon as my dad gets back, I'll tell him everything. In the meantime, I need to stay as close to the crown princess as possible."

"I will be with her this morning at a private function," Rosie said, thinking aloud. "You will not be able to join us. But I believe we both have some free time this afternoon. Maybe we can both talk to her, persuade her that she may be in grave danger. I understand where she is coming from, Carter. When you are in her position, you do not want to believe that those you have let into your inner circle could ever betray you."

Carter grinned at her friend. "See? And that's why you're the queen. You make the most excellent executive decisions."

Rosie's brown eyes twinkled. "I do try."

"Cannonball!" Carter shrieked, then jumped into the clear blue water.

Rosie giggled before performing an elegant swan dive, her body slicing effortlessly through the water. When she surfaced, she swam over to join the crown princess. Alice Catherine was at the edge of the pool, resting her chin on her hand.

Rosie had convinced Alice Catherine to meet her and Carter at the hotel's beautiful

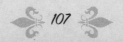

indoor pool, which the hotel staff voluntarily closed to guests for two hours to accommodate their royal visitors. Jorge sat at a table playing cards with Franz—one of Alice Catherine's personal security guards.

"It will be a good way to unwind before tonight's final event," Rosie had assured the princess. Ingrid had an appointment for a pedicure, and much to Carter's relief, chose not to cancel it. So, reluctantly, Alice Catherine had agreed to join them. She seemed to have forgiven Carter. But she wasn't having a lot of fun.

"I'm sorry, Rosie," she said. "I—I just can't stop thinking about what happened this morning."

"Please, Alice Catherine. Don't worry about it," Rosie told her, treading water. "How were you to know that your heel was going to break? Or that those shelves weren't stable?"

Alice Catherine closed her eyes, as if remembering each embarrassing moment. Carter had seen the whole thing on the news. Alice Catherine had joined Rosie, Nicholas, and Pavlos at an organic-foods store that provided surplus food to local shelters and schools for low-income children. But when she stepped back after making a short speech, her heel had broken. When she'd grabbed onto a shelf for support, the entire shelving unit had collapsed, sending marinara sauce and jars of olives smashing to the floor. Nicholas had tried to make a joke about the health benefits of not only eating but wearing Greek olives, but it hadn't been that funny. Especially to the people covered in red-wine-vinegar brine and chunks of tomato.

"You are just being kind. It was a disaster," Alice Catherine said with a moan.

Carter stopped in midlap. She wanted so

badly for Alice Catherine to believe her. But she didn't want to make her angry. "The press can be really cruel," she said, commiserating. "But people here in the U.S. love you, Your Highness. Some silly video on a Web site isn't going to change that."

Alice Catherine shook her head so fast that droplets flew from her hair. "You do not know my parents, Carter. There is no way that my less-than-successful public appearances have escaped their scrutiny. This is my first official *unaccompanied* visit. And probably my last."

"Okay. No getting around that you are looking kind of bad," Carter said. "But it's not your fault. Someone is behind all this. And we have very good reason to believe it's—"

Alice Catherine shoved off from the side and began doing the backstroke across the pool, effectively cutting off Carter. "You talked me into coming here to unwind," she called, not missing a beat. "Now . . . anyone up for a race?"

"This is almost as hot as a July day back home," Carter said from her spot on a low bench. She poured water from a pitcher onto the sauna rocks, loving the sizzle of the steam as it shot up. Then, she situated herself back against the sauna's redwood walls, a fluffy white towel wrapped around her. "Now if we only had some crawfish and fried green tomatoes and some Cajun music to dance to, it'd be just about perfect."

By the time the girls had swum three races, showed each other their silliest jumps, and found out who could hold their breath the longest underwater (Rosie, by fourteen seconds), Alice Catherine had come around a little. She still wouldn't hear a bad word spoken about Ingrid, but at least a smile had returned to her face.

"That does sound good," Alice Catherine said wistfully from beside Carter. "I would love to visit Louisiana one day."

Rosie nodded. "The beautiful bayous and swamps, the sunsets, the delicious food and amazing music. Not to mention the nicest people I've ever met. Louisiana is truly one of my favorite places in the world." Then she winked. "Besides this sauna. You should join me up here. It's even hotter on the high bench."

"I'm fine where I am, thanks," Carter said with a contented sigh as the heat rolled over her. They'd been in there almost fifteen minutes.

"In my country, saunas are quite popular," Alice Catherine told them. "Sometimes people leave the sauna, run out to roll in the snow, and then return to the sauna. They say it's very refreshing!"

Carter made a face. "That sounds like

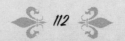

torture." As much as she had enjoyed herself, she was starting to feel pretty hot. "I think I'm going to go out and take a dip in the pool."

She pulled on the door handle. It wouldn't budge. "That's funny. It's stuck."

Rosie turned to look at the door. Her gaze caught the thermometer posted to the right side of it. "Carter, look! The thermostat is going up."

Alice Catherine hopped up from the bench and tried tugging on the handle as well. But even with two of them pulling on the door, it wouldn't move. And it was getting hotter by the second.

"Okay, let's not panic," Carter said, her heart racing. But she wasn't paying attention to her own advice. Because inside, her heart dropped into her stomach. The door wasn't just *stuck*. It was *locked*. And if they didn't get out of there fast, they could get dehydrated.

Nauseous. Maybe even . . . No, she didn't want to think about that.

Carter wiped the perspiration from her forehead, trying to think on her feet. The four walls of the room suddenly felt stifling and close. The sauna was located adjacent to the hotel pool. Carter peered out the tiny glass window. The place was deserted.

"I'm not feeling so well," Alice Catherine said, her eyelids fluttering. "I need—I need fresh air." Her words were coming slowly. "I feel like . . . I might . . . faint."

Rosie looked frightened. She yanked frantically at the door. "Carter! We have to get out of here!" She began banging on the door. "Where are the guards? Jorge! Franz!"

Carter slammed her fist again and again on the door. "Help!" she cried. "Help us!"

Rosie's hand reached for hers, and Carter felt her body sag against the door in defeat. This wasn't how she imagined her

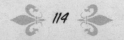

life ending—trapped in a hotel sauna with her best friend and a princess. . . .

And then, as if in a dream, the sauna door they were leaning against flew open. A burst of fresh air hit the girls as they stumbled out into the light.

"Dad!" Carter croaked.

Chapter 9

*T*he next few minutes were a blur. Mr. Mason and a group of other agents helped the girls out of the sauna and over to the cushioned lounge chairs that surrounded the pool. More security personnel than Carter had ever seen before in her life swarmed the area. Medics were called to check the girls' vital signs. Hotel staff rushed in with cool washcloths and bottles of water. A drowsy but going-to-be-okay Jorge and Franz were tended to. Someone had slipped a dose of allergy medicine into their iced teas, knocking them out for a couple of hours.

Mr. Mason knelt down beside Carter's

chair, a serious expression on his face. "Why don't you fill me in on what's been going on since I left, Carter? Because that door wasn't stuck. It was dead-bolted."

Carter swallowed. She felt as if she were about to be in a lot of trouble, but at least she didn't have to carry the burden of watching out for Alice Catherine on her own anymore.

She told her father everything, beginning with the text message and ending with her and Rosie's desperate attempt to get out of the sauna.

Her father heaved a sigh. "Didn't I make myself clear at homecoming that you should always come to me when there's a problem?"

Carter nodded, taking a swig of water. "But, Dad, you disappeared during the dinner. And then my phone was smashed and . . ." When she saw the look on her

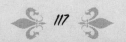

father's face, Carter stopped talking. "Sorry," she said. "No excuses."

He leaned over and kissed her forehead. "I just—I don't know what I'd do if anything happened to you." Then he turned to look over at Rosie and Alice Catherine, recuperating on the chairs next to Carter. "Or you, Your Highnesses."

Carter beamed. "What can I say, Dad? Saving princesses runs in the family."

"Another slice?" Carter offered, sliding the pizza box across the bed.

When the girls had finished giving their statements, Mr. Mason had escorted Rosie and Alice Catherine back to their hotel rooms. Agents waited outside while they each showered and changed. Then, taking no chances, the agents escorted Rosie and Alice Catherine to the Masons' hotel suite, where Carter had also showered and changed. She was lounging in her cozy fleece pants and a long sleeved tee when they arrived. All the while, Mr. Mason had been simultaneously on his laptop and on the phone with the Director of the Princess Protection Program, giving her an up-to-the-minute briefing on what had gone down.

Rosie helped herself to the pizza. "Mmm, my favorite. Pepperoni and mushroom." Other than nibbling on a piece of pepperoni, Alice Catherine had barely touched the slice in front of her. The day's events were obviously weighing on her.

"So, Your Highnesses. Carter," Mr. Mason said as he walked into Carter's room. "There's something you all need to know. Number one, we—meaning myself, the president and first lady, and the entire Princess Protection Program—are very, very thankful that you are all okay."

"Princess Protection Program?" Alice

Catherine repeated, looking confused.

"We'll fill you in later," Carter whispered, excited at the idea that the leader of the free world actually cared that *she*—an ordinary girl—was okay. "Go on, Dad." Then she saw how grim his expression was. "I, uh, think."

"Thankful—and angry that you once again got yourself involved in another international incident, Carter," he continued. "Because that 'something that came up' that pulled me away from the dinner?" He looked over at the crown princess. "It was because of you, Your Highness."

"Please, Major Mason," Alice Catherine said, her voice trembling, "tell me."

"The Director received a tip that pointed to a possible takeover of the throne in Scandia. Further intel pointed to a potential threat to the king and the young prince."

"My father? Peter?" Alice Catherine gasped. "Is my family okay?"

"The palace has been verified as secured," Mr. Mason assured her. "But, Your Highness, the intel that prompted my departure turned out to be incomplete. The danger posed was not to your family back in Scandia, as we had originally believed—but to you. I am very sorry to tell you that the danger comes not from an unknown enemy, but from someone you have known your entire life."

"So do you know who sent that text message, Dad?" Carter asked.

"They're working on it at headquarters," he answered. "We'll know soon enough."

"Thank you, Major Mason. And thank you, Queen Rosie. And . . ." Alice Catherine turned tearfully to Carter. "Thank you, Carter. I am sorry that I was so stubborn. All you wanted to do was help me. And—

and I was too blind to see the truth."

Carter impulsively reached over the pizza box and gave her a quick hug. "No problem, Your Highness. What's important is that you're safe now. And everyone will know that all the crazy things that have happened on your visit weren't your fault. You were being sabotaged!"

Alice Catherine hugged her back tightly. "Yes. Make no mistake. I realize and appreciate that my safety, of course, is important," she said. "But what is even more important to me now is that my cousin has the chance to speak for herself. I want her to explain what on Earth could have possessed her to do such a thing."

"You mean, like, ask her if she has a diabolical plan to, uh, bump you off and take over the throne?" Carter blurted out with a laugh before she could stop herself. Rosie and her father shot her a look.

Alice Catherine picked up her slice of pizza and took a big bite. "Exactly."

Rosie and Carter stood on the lower steps of the Lincoln Memorial, baseball caps pulled down over their foreheads. All they could see around them was their increased security detail—Rosie's guards, Alice Catherine's guards, some Princess Protection Program agents, and Mr. Mason. But if you didn't know they were there, you wouldn't have noticed them at all. They were used to blending into their surroundings.

Inside the templelike structure, next to the huge statue of Abraham Lincoln, stood Alice Catherine. She waited alone, her hair blowing in the late-afternoon breeze. No press was there to photograph her or call out questions. Carter's father had "leaked" the rumor that she would be attending an opera performance at the Kennedy Center. Carter smiled, imagining the hordes of reporters scurrying around trying to find the princess.

As if on cue, a lone figure strode across the grounds from the direction of the Capitol. It was Ingrid, clad in gray pants and a crisp white shirt. She wore a tweed news-boy cap over her bob.

"It worked, Carter," Rosie whispered excitedly, keeping her chin down in case Ingrid looked their way. They had, with Mr. Mason's okay, sent her the following text message using a special secret-agent cell phone:

Lapofluxury: change of plans.
Meet me at the Lincoln Memorial.
5 p.m.

Sure, it had been a trick. But it was the only way the girls could think of to trap the princess. Carter watched out of the corner

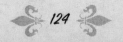

of her eye as Ingrid, a nervous expression on her face, walked up the dozens of steps and into the memorial itself. She thought she was about to meet whoever had sent her the directions via text, and she hadn't done what she'd been told to do—get rid of Alice Catherine.

Carter and Rosie quietly moved up the steps to get a better view. Carter pulled out the camera from her back pocket, her fingers fumbling for the buttons.

"Hello, Ingrid," Alice Catherine said to her cousin.

"Your Highness!" Ingrid said, looking totally shocked. She glanced around quickly, then turned back to face her cousin. "What are you doing here?"

"I think you're the one who needs to answer that question," Alice Catherine said softly. "I know what has been going on. You need to tell me the truth."

"The truth?" Ingrid rolled her blue eyes. "The truth is that my assistant must have gotten my schedule mixed up, because I was supposed to be meeting the mayor's daughter. I'm going to have to speak to her about that."

"Ingrid. Stop." The crown princess reached out and clasped her cousin's arm. "It's over. Please."

A smirk curled Ingrid's lips. "It's over?" She laughed bitterly. "How could it be over, cousin? You're still next in line, aren't you?"

Even though Alice Catherine could no longer deny the truth, hearing the words come directly from Ingrid's mouth definitely hurt. Carter could see her swallow. A flicker of pain flashed across her face. Then she drew herself up to her full height and stared Ingrid squarely in the eye. "I am next in line, Ingrid. Like it or not, that is our law. Peter will not be king, but he will join our military once his education is complete. He will make Scandia very proud."

"Gee, thanks for the history lesson," Ingrid said coldly.

Alice Catherine didn't take her eyes off her cousin or loosen her grip on her arm. "Ingrid, I have done nothing to deserve such treatment. Everything I have, I have shared with you. From our childhood to today, we have kept one another's confidences, sharing our hopes and dreams. But I cannot share the throne with you—nor should you want me to. You have many wonderful accomplishments in your own right."

Carter could see that Ingrid's spiteful facade was crumbling.

"Your landscape paintings are beautifully rendered," Alice Catherine went on. "You've inspired our country's youth to spend time outside hiking and riding bicycles and horseback riding. And since you have so much knowledge of ecology, our country's experts are eager to have your opinions and to work with you on Scandia's green initiatives."

Ingrid had begun to cry. She sank down on one of the steps, and Alice Catherine finally let go of her arm.

"I can't believe it," Carter whispered to Rosie. "She does have a heart after all."

"Shhh," Rosie said, still listening intently.

Alice Catherine sat down beside Ingrid and took her cousin's hand. "Please, Ingrid, tell me why you have tried to hurt me."

"I—I never wanted to do any of it," Ingrid said between sobs. "It was—I mean, I just thought that if people thought you weren't able to handle all your royal duties that maybe you would lose the chance to be queen." She sniffled. "And I know it sounds crazy and far-fetched, but that maybe then I would get to be queen in your place." She buried her face in her hands. "I never wanted to hurt you. Mother just said—"

Carter and Rosie gasped in unison. Ingrid's mother—the duchess—was Lapofluxury!

Ingrid's hands flew to her mouth, realizing that she had just spilled the beans.

"I never thought you wanted that life for yourself," Alice Catherine protested.

"I didn't," Ingrid admitted tearfully. "But Mother did. She just felt that if Peter lost the right to be king, the throne should be up for grabs—that it was just as much my right as it was yours. And I just wanted her to be happy." She gazed out at the reflecting pool, watching the sunlight dance across the water. "Father is going to be devastated when he finds out what we've done." She took a big gulp of air. "I did find it unfair that Peter had the throne taken away from him . . . but I lost sight of the fact that you would be losing out on being queen if my selfishness succeeded."

She looked at the crown princess, tears flowing down her face. "Can you ever find it in your heart to forgive me?"

Alice Catherine threw her arms around her cousin. "I already have."

Carter and Rosie allowed the princesses to have their moment together underneath Lincoln's steady gaze. They had captured the whole exchange on video with Carter's camera. *Not that we need it,* Carter thought as she watched the cousins tearfully embrace. Because for the first time since she had met the princesses, she could tell that they *both* were ready to do the right thing.

Chapter 10

"This is so cool," Carter whispered to Rosie as they walked down the carpeted hallway past yet another beautifully decorated room. "I can't believe you made this happen."

Rosie winked. "Being queen does have its privileges, you know." As a special surprise—and thank you—to Carter for not only being an awesome guest but managing to avert an international crisis, Rosie had arranged for a private tour of the White House. Mr. Mason had to finish up some business for the Princess Protection Program, so the girls were on their own.

Rosie had gone completely all-American.

She wore a white denim skirt and a navy blue T-shirt, with a bright red sweater tied around her neck. Her long hair was tied back with a red, white, and blue scarf, and she wore strappy red sandals.

When she found out where they were going, Carter did the best she could with what clean clothes were left in her suitcase—jeans, white shirt, and a tiny American-flag pin she'd bought on a whim from a souvenir stand outside the hotel.

"I was here once years ago with my dad. But that was for the self-guided public tour of the White House that regular American citizens can go on. We sure didn't get to come back here to the *real* White House," Carter said with a smile.

Being behind the scenes in the executive mansion was like having a window on to a secret world. The place was mind-boggling. There was a tennis court, a jogging track, a beautiful pool, and a movie theater. And if you lived in the White House, you didn't need to rent DVDs. Movies that were still playing in local theaters came to you in your own private theater.

That might just be the best perk of all, Carter decided as they walked past a room that looked as if it could be a family room. The furniture was very nice, but not quite as formal and stuffy as a lot of the rooms they had passed. There were two slip-covered khaki couches with tons of pillows, some worn leather armchairs, and a large flat-screen TV on the wall. A big coffee table with a chess set in midgame and a bowl of pretzels was in the middle of the room.

"Maybe that's where the Secret Service hangs out when they're on a break," she whispered to Rosie. Then an idea came to her and she grabbed Rosie's arm. "Or maybe that's where the first family hangs out."

Their tour guide, Meg—an efficient young woman wearing a dark pantsuit—turned to smile at them. "They were playing video games in there last weekend."

Carter gaped. "That is so cool."

"Want to grab a pretzel as a souvenir?" Meg asked. It was only when an exasperated Rosie yanked her back that Carter realized the guide was joking.

"Don't forget that this house is also very much a home," Meg said as they rounded a corner at the end of a corridor. "There are people here around the clock. But thanks to Teddy Roosevelt, the president's private quarters are off-limits to all but a select group. The first family's privacy is something we all respect."

"The president promised me that the next time I visit we will bowl together in the White House bowling alley," Rosie said, her face lighting up. "I love bowling. Remember,

Carter?" She turned to Meg. "The bowling alley in Lake Monroe is amazing. The music, the fried food, the colorful shoes, the sparkly balls." She sighed at the memory.

Carter laughed. "Only you could make bowling sound like more fun than a day at the beach."

Rosie pretended to look shocked. "You think a day at the beach can even compare to the great American sport of bowling?"

Meg had promised to take them to the kitchen, where rumor was, some very delicious gingerbread was going to be made that afternoon. People bustled down the hallway, all looking very official—but in a friendly way. Carter thought it seemed like a very exciting place to work. Maybe one day, she thought, wondering how good your grades had to be to get a job at the White House. She'd completed all her French assignments yesterday, spent this morning working on her math homework, and she'd finish reading the novel for English class on the plane home. The only subject she hadn't focused on much was history.

Which was pretty ironic, really. I would definitely get an A if my teacher could see me now, she thought, walking past an oil painting of an older man looking very presidential with his gray hair, black coat, and stiff, high white collar.

"James Buchanan," Meg said, glancing up at the portrait. "The only president who never got married."

A bachelor for president? Carter thought that was a little sad. Being the president had to be incredibly hard. And how lonely would it be if you had no one to share things with at the end of the day?

Unless you had amazing friends. I hope you had a BFF, James, Carter thought as they walked by. She glanced over at Rosie,

who gave her a big smile back. I hope you were as lucky as I am.

"That was the best, Rosie. Thank you so much," Carter told her friend. It really had been a once-in-a-lifetime chance to be up close and personal with history—and to taste some knock-your-socks-off gingerbread.

After they had finished their tour and thanked Meg a million times, a black sedan that would take them to the airport was waiting in the driveway in front of the White House.

Rosie would be flying back to Costa Luna via private jet. Carter would be meeting her dad at the airport—and flying economy back to Louisiana.

"I enjoyed it very much, Carter. I loved seeing the president's desk and imagining all the exciting business that takes place there."

"Me, too." Carter paused. "But what I really meant was thanks for the whole trip. Everything. This was a really important trip for you, and it was amazing that you asked me to be a part of it."

"It wouldn't have been half as much fun without you," Rosie said. "And if it hadn't been for you, who knows what would have happened to Alice Catherine? Thanks to you, the crown princess is safe." Carter and Rosie had said their good-byes to Alice Catherine earlier that morning. She would be flying back to Scandia that night with Ingrid. She had promised to stand by her cousin as she and the duchess faced their fate.

Carter had a feeling that the king would be proud of his daughter—and hoped, now that he knew the whole story, that he wouldn't be too hard on Ingrid. As for Ingrid's mother, the duchess, well . . . Carter was sure she'd be reading about that royal mess for weeks to come.

Hey! That's the perfect topic for my history paper, Carter thought. Succession: What's the Fair Solution?

"There's just one more thing," Rosie said, reaching into her monogrammed tote bag and pulling out a small black leather case.

Carter gasped as she opened the case. It was a new cell phone engraved with Carter's name! And being the amazing friend that she was, Rosie had already programmed the address book with all of Carter's important numbers and given her a cool ring tone.

"You are the best, Rosie," Carter said, already testing the features. "How can I pay you back?"

Rosie bit her lip. "Well . . . I know you will think I am crazy. But if you could send me a pair of my own bowling shoes? That would be incredible."

Carter reached over and gave Rosie a fist bump. "Yeah, you are crazy. That's why I love you!"

"Promise me that the next time we see each other, we'll spend more time together," Rosie said, looking out the window as the sedan whizzed down the D.C. highway. "No missions."

"And no state duties," Carter told her.

The two best friends stared at each other—then burst into laughter.

"Right. Who are we kidding?" Carter said.

"But that is the sign of true friendship," Rosie said, resting her head on Carter's shoulder. "Being able to be yourself. So even if I'm meeting with the ambassador to France—"

"And I'm saving a princess from the brink of disaster—" Carter began.

Rosie smiled. "We always will make time—"

"For each other," they finished together.

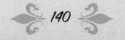

Don't miss the next book in the Princess
Protection Program series

Royalty UNDERCOVER

By Wendy Loggia

Based on "Princess Protection Program," Teleplay by Annie DeYoung

Based on the Story by David Morgasen and Annie DeYoung

*C*arter Mason is flying to Costa Luna to visit her
best friend, the queen! She's looking forward to a
week in the sun and some good old-fashioned
F-U-N. But Queen Rosalinda is busy planning her
country's Independence Day festivities. Plus, she
has another guest at the palace—Princess Natalie, a
young girl whose identity needs to stay secret.
Carter offers to keep an eye on the little princess.
But when Natalie pushes her to her limit, Carter
blurts out a little white lie. Before Carter can tell
Natalie the truth, the cutest boy she's ever seen
comes over to talk to her. And he thinks she's a
princess. What's a girl to do?